No Tiff!

Written by Alex Marson
Illustrated by Natalie Merheb

Collins

Tiff hits Ted off.

Ben picks him up.

3

Tiff has a big bat.

Tiff hits Ted off.

Ben pops Ted back up.

Tiff tips and kicks.

Tiff kicks Ted back off.

Ben huffs and puffs.

Ben is a bit sad.

Tiff picks up the bag.

The big bag can fit.

Ted fits in the bag!

/f/

14

ff

15

After reading

Letters and Sounds: Phase 2

Word count: 56

Focus phonemes: /g/ /o/ /c/ /k/ ck /e/ /u/ /h/ /b/ /f/ ff

Common exception words: has, and, the, is, no

Curriculum links: Physical development; Personal, social and emotional development

Early learning goals: Reading: read and understand simple sentences; use phonic knowledge to decode regular words and read them aloud accurately; read some common irregular words; demonstrate understanding when talking with others about what they have read

Developing fluency

- Your child may enjoy hearing you read the book.
- Take turns to read a page. Encourage your child to read with expression. Demonstrate how to emphasise the speech bubble on page 5 to show how Ben is warning Tiff to be careful.

Phonic practice

- Remind your child that two letters can make one sound. On page 2, point to and sound out **Tiff** (T/i/ff), focusing your child on how the double "ff" makes one sound (/f/).
- On page 6, point to and sound out **back** (b/a/ck), pointing out how "ck" makes one sound (/c/). Ask your child to read page 7, looking out for where two letters make one sound. (*Tiff, kicks*)
- Look at the "I spy sounds" pages (14 and 15). Point to the frog on page 15 and then the /f/ at the top of page 14. Say: I spy a /f/ in frog. Challenge your child to point to and name different things they can see containing the /f/ sound. (e.g. *flowers, fox, fork, fish, frog, fruit, flamingo, football, Tiff , earmuffs, giraffe, daffodils*) You could ask your child about spellings, e.g. ask: Which word has the letters f and f which make the /f/ sound? Prompt by pointing to Tiff and asking: What is the girl's name? (*Tiff*)

Extending vocabulary

- Focus on page 7. Discuss the two things Tiff does. (*tips, kicks*) Ask: What can you kick? (e.g. *I can kick a ball*) What can you tip? (e.g. *I can tip a bottle*)
- Discuss other simple action words. Take turns to mime an action, saying: I can do this (then mime, e.g. *turn, lean, throw, lift, drop, catch*), whilst the other guesses what the action is.